Special thanks to
Sarah Levison

ORCHARD BOOKS

First published in 2016 by The Watts Publishing Group

3 5 7 9 10 8 6 4 2

A CIP catalogue record for this book is available from the British Library.

ISBN 978 1 40834 157 5

Printed and bound in China

The paper and board used in this book are made from wood from responsible sources

Orchard Books
An imprint of Hachette Children's Group
Part of The Watts Publishing Group Limited
Carmelite House, 50 Victoria Embankment, London EC4Y 0DZ

An Hachette UK Company
www.hachette.co.uk
www.hachettechildrens.co.uk

Pinkie Pie's Perfect Party

ORCHARD

Pinkie Pie gives the best parties EVER and loves to make everyone laugh and have fun. Her cutie mark is three bouncing balloons.

Cheese Sandwich is a mysterious new pony. He says he is the best party planner in Equestria! His cutie mark is a sandwich.

Princess Celestia is the ruler of all Equestria. She is beautiful, kind and wise. Her cutie mark is a sun.

Twilight Sparkle is learning all about magic. Her cutie mark is a pink star.

Rarity is a glamorous unicorn. Her cutie mark is three blue diamonds.

Fluttershy is very quiet and shy. She loves animals. Her cutie mark is three pink butterflies.

Rainbow Dash is a fast Pegasus pony. She helps to control the weather. Her cutie mark is a cloud with a rainbow lightning bolt.

Applejack works on a farm. Her cutie mark is three red apples.

Contents

PART ONE
Party Plans

Chapter One

Pinkie the Party Pony

Pinkie Pie sang happily to herself as she trotted into Ponyville. She was planning a party and she needed to buy some important party things!

Pinkie Pie threw the most amazing parties in Ponyville.

She gave brilliant birthday parties, super sleepovers and fantastic fancy-dress parties. Pinkie Pie always made sure that all her friends had the best time.

Pinkie Pie went from stall to stall and bought streamers, glitter, paint and balloons. All the ponies in Ponyville loved seeing Pinkie because she was always happy.

"Today's party is going to be the best one yet!" Pinkie Pie told a stallholder.

When she got back to her house at Sugarcube Corner, Applejack, Rarity, Twilight Sparkle and all her best friends were waiting for her. They were very excited to hear about the party she was planning.

With her friends' help, Pinkie uscd rainbow-coloured paints to make a huge banner.

The party was a birthday party for Rainbow Dash!

"This is going to be SO much fun!" Applejack said.

"Yay!" cried Fluttershy.

Pinkie Pie gave Rainbow Dash an enormous hug. "Rainbow Dash, you have my Pinkie Party Promise that you will have the best birthday party EVER! Who's ready to plan a super duper PARTY?!"

Before Pinkie's friends could respond, a deep voice replied, "I am!"

The ponies caught sight of a new pony standing in the shadows. Who was this mysterious stranger?

Chapter Two

The Birthday Plan

"My name is Cheese Sandwich, and I'm the best party planner in all Equestria," the pony said, walking towards the friends. He was wearing a cowboy hat and he had a rubber chicken riding on his back!

"Well, my name is Pinkie Pie and I'm planning a party!" said Pinkie Pie happily.

Rainbow Dash was delighted that there were TWO ponies to organise her party. "This is going to be brilliant!" she said.

Rainbow Dash gave Pinkie Pie and Cheese Sandwich a hug. "It'll be the best birthday party EVER with both of you planning it!"

Cheese Sandwich threw off his hat and sang a lively song.

He told everyone that he was a
super party pony.

Pinkie Pie felt a bit left
out. After all, everyone knew
she planned the parties in
Ponyville. She didn't really
want another pony helping her.

Cheese Sandwich and the other ponies galloped off to the town square to start getting everything ready for the party.

Pinkie Pie was left alone. "But what about me?" she asked sadly.

All her friends seemed to
have forgotten about her now
that Cheese Sandwich was
in town!

Chapter Three

The Big Cheese

In the town square, Cheese
Sandwich started to organise
Rainbow Dash's party. A
huge picture of the birthday
pony hung above a stage and
there were pretty rainbow
decorations in all the trees.

Best of all, there was delicious food and drink everywhere.

"This is going to be a brilliant party!" Rainbow Dash said to Cheese Sandwich.

Back at Sugarcube Corner, Pinkie Pie was feeling very sad.

Her good friend Twilight Sparkle trotted by. "Pinkie, aren't you going to help plan the party?" she asked.

But Pinkie Pie shook her head and pretended to be busy watering some plants.

She was too proud to admit that she felt upset and left out.

"If Cheese Sandwich really is the best party planner in town, then I'm not needed any more," Pinkie said to herself, her mane and tail drooping miserably.

Pinkie Pie put away her party cannon and her balloons. She wasn't needed as a party planner any more. What was she going to do?

PART TWO
The Return of Party Pinkie

Chapter One
Time for Action!

Pinkie Pie had a very sad day all on her own. Finally, she decided to look at some photographs of the parties she had organised. There were so many! There was Twilight Sparkle's welcome party,

then there was Gummy the
crocodile's birthday bash
and Princess Cadance's
wedding! Pinkie Pie began
to feel much more cheerful.
"We had lots of fun!" she
remembered happily.

Putting on her funniest costume, Pinkie Pie felt much better. She had to stop feeling sorry for herself and prove to everyone that SHE was the best party planner in the whole of Equestria!

Trotting into the town square, Pinkie Pie saw that Cheese Sandwich had already organised lots of special birthday treats for Rainbow Dash. There was a chocolate fountain and a light display.

There was even a huge ice sculpture in the shape of Rainbow Dash's cutie mark! Pinkie Pie thought that he had done a very good job.

All her friends thought so too. As Pinkie got closer she heard

Applejack talking to Cheese.

"You really are a brillant party planner!" cried Applejack, giving him a hug.

Pinkie Pie felt very cross.

Cheese Sandwich had taken her job and now he was taking her friends! She had to stop him. And there was only one thing she could think of that might work…

Chapter Two

Pinkie Pie's Challenge

"Freeze, Cheese!" shouted Pinkie Pie, making all the ponies stop what they were doing. Pinkie Pie looked very cross! "Enough is enough. Cheese Sandwich, I challenge you to a silly contest!"

Applejack, Rarity, Rainbow
Dash and Twilight Sparkle
looked at each other. That
sounded serious…even though
none of them knew what a silly
contest was!

Cheese Sandwich smiled as
he agreed to Pinkie's challenge.

"You really think that you can be sillier than me?" he scoffed.

"I know I can!" replied Pinkie Pie. "And the winner of the silly contest gets to plan Rainbow Dash's birthday party!"

As Cheese Sandwich and Pinkie Pie got dressed in their silliest outfits, Twilight Sparkle explained the rules. The contestants needed to perform in the silliest, wackiest, wildest and funniest way they could.

The pony who made the judge laugh the most would win!

Twilight Sparkle decided that Rainbow Dash should judge the competition. After all, the winner would be in charge of organising her birthday party!

Rainbow Dash didn't really want to judge the competition. She knew that whoever lost would be unhappy…but before she could say anything it was time for the contest to begin!

Chapter Three
The Silly Contest!

All the ponies in the town square felt very nervous as Cheese Sandwich and Pinkie Pie walked up to each other. What was going to happen next? The silly contest was about to begin!

Pinkie Pie and Cheese
Sandwich started being as silly
as they could be! First Pinkie
Pie put on a funny hat and
pulled faces. Then she balanced
on a bouncy ball, sang a silly
birthday song and juggled.

Then Cheese Sandwich
balanced on a huge cheese and
did a funny dance as he rolled
around!

Next, Pinkie Pie went up in
a hot-air balloon and caught
Rainbow with a fishing rod.

Finally, Cheese Sandwich danced a funny dance with Rainbow Dash, making her laugh and giggle out loud.

As the two ponies got sillier and sillier, the watching ponies looked on in delight.

Both the ponies were so funny, how would Rainbow Dash ever be able to pick a winner?

Next, Cheese Sandwich brought out a giant party cannon and fired Rainbow Dash high into the air.

Pinkie Pie knew that she had to do something even more special. She produced an enormous rainbow-coloured cake! But the cake was so heavy that the rope carrying it snapped!

The enormous cake fell on top of Rainbow Dash, trapping the poor pony beneath it. Pinkie Pie gasped in horror. Was Rainbow Dash OK?

PART THREE
Pinkie Pie's Perfect Party

Chapter One

Pinkie's Party Promise

The ponies all rushed to help
Rainbow Dash. Luckily she
wasn't hurt.

But as Pinkie Pie watched
her friend struggle out from
underneath the cake, she
realised something awful.

She had broken the Pinkie Party Promise!

Earlier that day she had promised Rainbow Dash that she would have the best party ever. But Rainbow Dash wasn't having fun at all. Pinkie Pie knew she had to do something!

"The silly contest is over!" she cried. "I give up. Cheese wins. He can plan Rainbow Dash's birthday party."

Pinkie Pie walked away sadly. If she left, Cheese could organise a magical party.

Best of all, Rainbow Dash would have a wonderful time for her birthday.

Later that day, Pinkie Pie finished packing her belongings. She had decided to leave Ponyville. Just then, she heard someone call out, "Pinkie, wait!" Turning around, there were all of her friends.

Rainbow Dash flew in front of Pinkie Pie, blocking her path. "I'm so sorry that we made you feel left out!" she cried.

"We all are," agreed Twilight.

"I'm sorry that I stopped you having the best birthday ever!" said Pinkie Pie.

All the ponies hugged Pinkie Pie. "You and Cheese Sandwich are BOTH great party planners," Rainbow Dash said.

"Cheese Sandwich is a great guest planner. But you are our best friend. We could never have a party without you!"

Chapter Two
The Cheese Reveal

Just then, Cheese Sandwich appeared. He stepped forward and took off his hat. "Rainbow Dash is right," he said. "I never meant to take your place. I just wanted to show you how good I was at party planning."

"Why?" asked Pinkie Pie, feeling surprised.

Cheese Sandwich told the friends that when he was a young foal he was very shy. He didn't have any friends! He decided to leave his home and seek his destiny in Equestria.

Cheese Sandwich happened to pass through Ponyville one day when there was a party taking place. Everyone was so friendly and welcoming and full of fun and joy!

"That day changed my life," said Cheese Sandwich. "I decided that I would plan parties and travel around Equestria, helping everyone to have amazing parties."

"But what does all this have to do with me?" asked Pinkie Pie in confusion.

Cheese Sandwich hugged
Pinkie Pie. "You were the one
throwing the party that day in
Ponyville! You made me decide
to become a party planner!
Can we work together to plan
Rainbow Dash's party?"

All the ponies looked at
Pinkie Pie.

"You bet!" cried Pinkie Pie,
bouncing up and down happily.
"Let's party!"

Chapter Three
The Best Party EVER!

And so Cheese Sandwich and Pinkie Pie worked together to make sure that Rainbow Dash and everyone in Ponyville had the best party ever! There was music, dancing, a swimming pool, hippo rides and balloons.

And, of course, there was the biggest birthday cake anyone had ever seen!

"This party is brilliant!" Rainbow Dash told Pinkie Pie and Cheese Sandwich. "Thank you both very much."

"That's all I needed to hear, little filly," smiled Cheese. He gave Pinkie his rubber chicken and rode off into the sunset. It was time for him to go and help out at the next party, wherever that may be!

As Cheese Sandwich trotted out of Ponyville, Pinkie Pie and her best friends felt very happy. They'd made a special new friend, and Pinkie Pie had lots of amazing new ideas for future parties!

But, most importantly, Pinkie Pie now knew that working together made a party twice as fun!

The End

There's lots of colour, sticker and activity fun with My Little Pony!